Abraham's Great Love

By:
ouie T. McClain II

Melanin Origins

Published by Melanin Origins
PO Box 122123; Arlington, TX 76012
All rights reserved, including the right of reproduction in whole or in part in any form.

Copyright © 2022

First Edition

Series Editors: Reginald Robinson; Lenny Williams, & Shiree Fowler

Library of Congress Control Number: 2021942094

ISBN: 978-1-62676-513-9 hardback

ISBN: 978-1-62676-514-6 paperback

ISBN: 978-1-62676-515-3 ebook

This book is dedicated to all men in women around the world who recognize the value of a beautiful reflection. Regardless of race, color, or creed you press forward to express God's love to all of humanity. Thank you for your service, dedication, and for all that you do on behalf of the human family.

Louie T. McClain II

Long ago the LORD said to Abraham, "Get out of your country, and away from your kindred and your father's house to the land that I will show you. And I will make of you a great nation, and I will bless you and make your name great, so that you will be a blessing." Genesis 12:1-2

"So Abram departed, as the LORD had spoken unto him." Genesis 12:4

Scripture says God counted Abraham as a righteous man because of his belief in the unseen Creator of all things.

Yet, behind Abraham's faith, was his great love for God.

Love is a powerful feeling
of deep connection that
a person has for another
person or thing,

And the highest form of love is when care is focused on the greater good of another rather than oneself.

The life of Abraham, who is known as the Father of Many Nations, is one of the greatest examples of love that Scripture blesses us with.

9

In submission to God's will, Abraham left
everything that was normal in his life to
go after what God had in store for him.

When things got rough on his journey, he didn't turn back to go home. Out of his love for God, Abraham remained on the path towards his destiny.

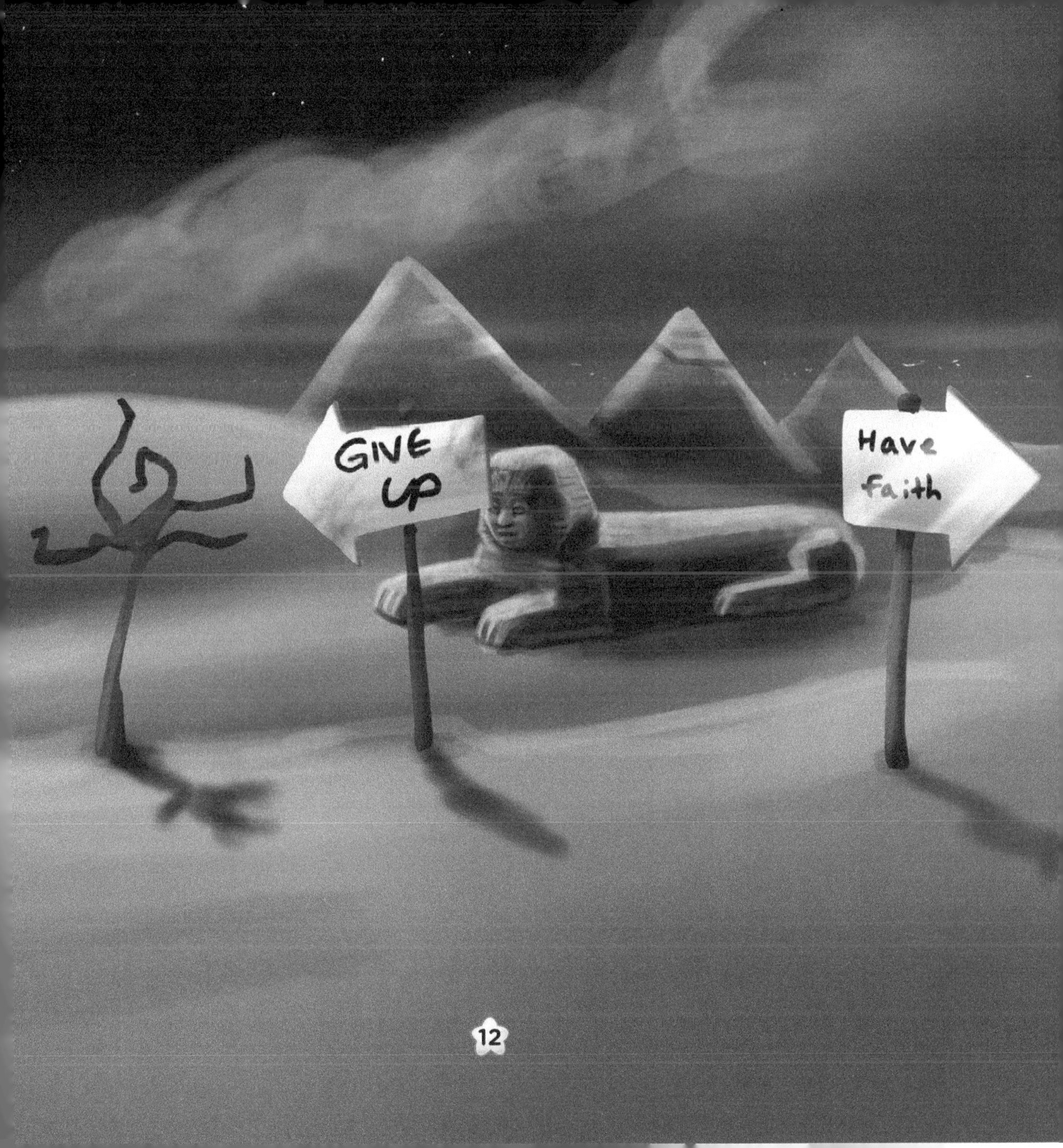
GIVE
UP
Have
Faith

God blesses the faithful. The Lord blessed Abraham so much along his journey that he and his nephew, Lot, had so many possessions that they were forced to part ways.

In a humble and loving spirit, Abraham gave his nephew the choice to decide which countryside he wanted to settle in first.

As Lot's elder, Abraham could have demanded to choose the best living area for himself, but Abraham was not concerned about that land. His love for God connected him to a greater purpose.

When God promised to give Abraham a son in his old age, he smiled in his heart and said, "Is anything too hard for the Lord?"

16

Abraham's life shows the spiritual connection he had with God, and it also reveals how his devotion to God extended to a love for God's creation.

Abraham sought fairness in all things with all people. He even begged the Lord not to destroy nearby cities that He was not pleased with.

"What if ten righteous men live there? Shall not the Judge of all the earth do right?" Abraham said to the Lord.

God listens to the prayers of those who come to Him in sincerity and in love.

The Lord also shows His love by honoring His promises like when He gave Abraham a child in his old age.

God demonstrates his great love towards everything He created by providing for our well-being each day.

For love is the way and God is love.
If you ever need a reminder about
how to treat others...

Think of the life of Abraham and how his great loving heart empowered him to be the best that God wanted him to be.

24

"I am the Almighty God; walk before me and be perfect." Genesis 17:1

Order Melanin Origins
ALL In All Series!

ALL IN ALL SERIES

www.MelaninOrigins.com

CPSIA information can be obtained
at www.ICGtesting.com
Printed in the USA
LVHW052053090921
697442LV00002B/69